PUFFIN BOOKS

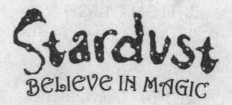

Stardust

BELIEVE IN MAGIC

Linda Chapman lives in Leicestershire with her family and two Bernese mountain dogs. She used to be a stage manager in the theatre. When she is not writing she spends her time looking after her two young daughters, horse riding and teaching drama.

Books by Linda Chapman

BRIGHT LIGHTS
CENTRE STAGE

My Secret Unicorn series
THE MAGIC SPELL
DREAMS COME TRUE
FLYING HIGH
STARLIGHT SURPRISE
STRONGER THAN MAGIC
A SPECIAL FRIEND
A WINTER WISH

Stardust series
MAGIC BY MOONLIGHT
BELIEVE IN MAGIC

Stardust

BELIEVE IN MAGIC

Linda Chapman

Illustrated by Biz Hull

PUFFIN

PUFFIN BOOKS

Published by the Penguin Group
Penguin Books Ltd, 80 Strand, London WC2R 0RL, England
Penguin Group (USA), Inc., 375 Hudson Street, New York, New York 10014, USA
Penguin Books Australia Ltd, 250 Camberwell Road, Camberwell, Victoria 3124, Australia
Penguin Books Canada Ltd, 10 Alcorn Avenue, Toronto, Ontario, Canada M4V 3B2
Penguin Books India (P) Ltd, 11 Community Centre, Panchsheel Park, New Delhi – 110 017, India
Penguin Books (NZ) Ltd, Cnr Rosedale and Airborne Roads, Albany, Auckland, New Zealand
Penguin Books (South Africa) (Pty) Ltd, 24 Sturdee Avenue, Rosebank 2196, South Africa

Penguin Books Ltd, Registered Offices: 80 Strand, London WC2R 0RL, England

www.penguin.com

First published 2005

4

Text copyright © Linda Chapman, 2005
Illustrations copyright © Biz Hull, 2005
All rights reserved

The moral right of the author and illustrator has been asserted

Set in Monotype Bembo

Made and printed in England by Clays Ltd, St Ives plc

Except in the United States of America, this book is sold subject to the condition that it shall not, by
way of trade or otherwise, be lent, re-sold, hired out, or otherwise circulated without the publisher's
prior consent in any form of binding or cover other than that in which it is published and without a
similar condition including this condition being imposed on the subsequent purchaser

British Library Cataloguing in Publication Data
A CIP catalogue record for this book is available from the British Library

ISBN 0–141–317809

For Tabitha and Hannah Piggott,
who sparkle with stardust

CHAPTER

One

The wind streamed through Lucy's long
chestnut brown hair. Stretching out her
arms, she twirled around in the sky so she
was floating on her back. The stars shone
down and the warm summer air seemed
to hug itself around her. Lucy stared
upwards at the glittering stars. It felt as
though they were reaching out to her,
calling her . . .

'Come on, slowcoach!'

Lucy blinked. Allegra Greenwood, her best friend, was swooping towards her. 'What are you doing, Luce?' she demanded. 'Come on!' Her blue eyes glinted teasingly. 'Bet you can't catch me!'

'Bet I can!' Lucy replied, reaching out to tag her friend.

But Allegra was as quick as a darting swallow. Dodging Lucy's outstretched hand, she shot up towards the stars, flying higher and higher.

Lucy followed, her heart racing with excitement. She was closing the gap on Allegra. This time she *was* going to catch her . . .

'*Got you!*' she gasped, tagging Allegra's left foot.

Allegra somersaulted in surprise. 'You've got faster!' she exclaimed.

Lucy grinned. Usually she only managed to tag Allegra when her friend got bored of flying in a straight line and began showing off by turning somersaults or pirouettes. *I'm getting better at flying*, Lucy thought with a surge of pride. However, she didn't want to sound boastful so she just shrugged. 'It was probably a fluke. You're loads quicker than me really.'

'Let's try again!' Allegra dived off into the sky.

As Lucy followed, she thought about how easily flying came to her now. It was almost impossible to believe that just a few months ago she hadn't known she could fly. She knew she would always remember the day Allegra had moved in next door – the day she had first found out about stardust.

She had stayed at Allegra's house that night and her new friend had told her how everyone in the world is made out of stardust. Some people, she had explained to Lucy, had more stardust than others. You could always spot them because they were very imaginative, loved animals and believed in magic. When the stars came out, these people could turn themselves into stardust spirits. Allegra was a stardust spirit and so, it turned out, was Lucy. Ever since then, Lucy had been living a secret stardust life after her parents and two older sisters had gone to bed.

It was great fun. She and Allegra met up every night in the woods with their two friends, Ella and Faye. As stardust spirits it was their job to help protect nature, putting right any problems caused by humans. They could fly and work magic, and the older stardust spirits gave them tasks to do.

As Lucy thought about Ella and Faye, she suddenly remembered that she and Allegra were supposed to be meeting them in the nearby hawthorn clearing.

'Whoops!' Lucy muttered. She called up to Allegra, 'We'd better go. Ella and Faye will be waiting.'

'I'll come in a minute,' Allegra called back as she twirled on one leg in the air. 'I just want to practise a new spin.'

Lucy swooped downwards. 'Sorry we're late,' she apologized as she reached the hawthorn clearing and landed by Ella and Faye.

'That's OK,' Ella said. 'We haven't been waiting long.' Ella was tall with long dark hair and brown eyes. She was wearing a green dress the colour of new leaves in spring.

Faye was much smaller. She had big blue eyes that matched her sapphire-blue dress and short blonde hair that fluffed out around her face. Both she and Ella were nine years old, just like Lucy and Allegra. 'Do you know what we're supposed to be doing this evening?' Faye asked Lucy.

'Checking on the water voles,' Lucy replied.

Just then, Allegra danced down to meet them. 'Hi, you guys. Look at my new spin. It's really cool!' She spun on one leg and turned a backflip to finish.

'Wow!' Faye said, impressed.

'Here, I'll teach you,' Allegra offered. 'Look, you just –'

'Shouldn't we go and check on the water voles if that's what we're supposed to be doing?' Ella interrupted.

Allegra shrugged. 'We'll go in a minute. I'll just show Faye how to do this spin.'

'No, come on, let's go now,' Lucy said. She knew what Allegra was like. She would get so involved in teaching Faye the new spin that they would all still be there half an hour later. Seeing an argumentative frown start to cross Allegra's face, she dived upwards into the sky. 'Can't catch me!'

Allegra leapt to the challenge just as Lucy had hoped. 'Says who?' she cried, flying upwards and tagging Lucy's foot in one swift movement. 'Got you!' She giggled. 'Come on, let's find the water voles. I don't know what you lot are waiting for!'

It could be very exhausting keeping up with Allegra, Lucy reflected as they flew to the riverbank. Allegra was constantly flitting from one wild idea to another and was never still for a moment. But she was a brilliant best friend. Now the summer holidays had started and the weather was so hot, Lucy imagined the days stretching out ahead of them, spent lazing in the gardens of their two houses, playing with her rabbit, Thumper, and generally having fun.

She increased her speed and caught up with Allegra. 'Now it's the holidays we'll have to have loads of sleepovers at each other's houses.'

'Definitely,' Allegra agreed. 'Ask your mum if you can come over and stay tomorrow.'

'You two are so lucky living next door to each other,' Ella said enviously. She and Faye lived in the nearby town. They went to the same school as each other, but they weren't next-door neighbours like Lucy and Allegra.

'I know,' Lucy replied. It made meeting up at night very easy.

Lucy often wondered what her mum and dad would say if they ever found out what she got up to after they'd gone to bed. It was very hard keeping it secret from them. When she went out flying, she put a pillow under her duvet so if they looked into her room it seemed as if she was still there. She hoped they would never check too closely. Allegra was lucky; her mum, Xanthe, was a stardust spirit and went out flying at night too.

'There's the river!' Ella said, interrupting Lucy's thoughts.

Faye frowned. 'The water level's very low.'

'It's because it's been so hot,' Lucy said. For the last three weeks there had been a heatwave.

They landed beside the steep riverbank. The river was running very sluggishly, bits of litter floating in the slow-moving water. A colony of voles lived in the bank in a warren of tunnels. Their entrances were usually hidden from sight by the thick reeds and vegetation that grew over the bank, but that night they could be clearly seen. Lucy frowned. 'Look, you can see the voles' burrows. It must be because the water level's dropped.'

Allegra looked worried. 'If we can see them so can any passing fox or stoat or other animal who might be looking for food.'

'We should do something,' Ella said. 'Water voles are quite rare.'

'I know: I'll conjure some rain,' Faye suggested, raising her hands.

'No, don't!' Lucy said quickly. 'The river's low because of the hot weather. That's part of nature so we can't use magic to fix it.'

'Of course,' Faye said, lowering her hands. 'You're right, Lucy.' The others nodded. They all knew that stardust spirits were only allowed to use their magic to solve problems caused by people. They

weren't ever allowed to use their powers
to interfere with nature.

'There must be something we can do to
help,' Allegra said. 'Even if we can't use
magic.'

Lucy crouched down and looked at the
burrows. How *could* they help the voles?
Two black whiskers poked out of one of
the holes. 'Look,' she whispered.

They all stayed very still. The whiskers
were followed by a nose. It twitched
several times and then a round-cheeked,
hamster-like head appeared. Fluffy brown
fur framed two dark, bright eyes. Holding
her breath, Lucy leant forward and held
out her cupped hands. The vole's whiskers
trembled and then he scampered out of
the burrow. Sitting up on Lucy's hands, he
looked around. He was the size of a very

large mouse and his body felt heavy and
warm.

'He's gorgeous,' Allegra breathed.

Lucy kissed him very gently on the
nose and then placed him back in the
entrance of his burrow. She really wanted
to help him and the other voles. 'We could
always pick some reeds and cover up the
holes with them. We won't be using our

magic so it's OK and it might help hide
the burrows a bit.'

'Good idea!' Ella said eagerly.

Jumping to their feet, they all began to
cover the holes. The reeds were stiff and
Lucy could feel them cutting into her
hands but she didn't care. Protecting the
voles was more important.

'The river's flowing very slowly tonight,
isn't it?' Faye commented as they worked.
'And look over there! Is that oil or
something on the surface?'

Lucy followed her gaze. Just upstream,
where the river came round a bend, there
was an ugly sheen on the water. 'I think it
is oil,' she said. The dark patch was
gradually creeping its way towards them.

Allegra frowned. 'I wonder where it's
coming from. I'll fly upstream and see if I

can find out.'

She flew off and came back a minute later looking very worried. 'Someone's dumped a load of rubbish in the river just around the bend. Come and see.'

The four of them flew upstream. A large pile of rubbish was blocking the river: an old mattress, some cushions, three bin bags spilling over with hedge trimmings and two oil cans. Lucy saw some tyre marks on the nearby track. 'Someone must have driven down here in a car or a van and just dumped all this rubbish!' she said in alarm.

'We're going to have to do something,' Ella said quickly. 'The oil is already spreading downstream. If it reaches the water voles it might poison them. Look, it's already killed a fish.' She pointed to

where a fish's small silver body was
floating, belly up, near the reeds.

'What can we do?' asked Faye.

Ideas raced through Lucy's head. Each
girl was a different type of stardust spirit
and they were all able do different types of
magic. She was a summer spirit, which
meant that she could warm things up or
start fires – obviously no good when there
was oil around. Allegra, an autumn spirit,
could make the wind blow but she wasn't
very good at controlling which way it
blew and it might just make the oil move
towards the voles even more quickly. Faye,
who was a winter spirit, could make it
rain and Ella, a spring spirit, could make
things grow, but Lucy couldn't see how
either of those powers would help stop the
oil reaching the voles.

'We need to get help,' she said. 'We can't deal with this on our own.'

Allegra nodded, looking serious for once. 'You're right. Come on, let's go!'

The four friends flew as fast as they could
to the clearing in the centre of the woods
where the stardust spirits met every night.
Allegra had told Lucy that all around the
world, stardust spirits gathered in such
glades, choosing the oldest tree in the
woods as their meeting point.

In the clearing that night there were
about twenty stardust spirits. Some were

sitting in the trees talking and laughing, others were flying through the air, their green, blue, gold and silver clothes shining in the starlight. Looking around, Lucy saw Xanthe, Allegra's mum, chatting to some of the other stardust spirits by the huge, gnarled oak tree that stood in the middle of the glade. She felt a rush of relief. Xanthe would know what to do. Swooping down, Lucy landed beside her.

'What's the matter?' Xanthe asked, seeing her worried face.

'The river. It's got oil in it,' Lucy panted.

'It's near the voles,' Allegra said, landing beside her. 'We don't know what to do.'

'All right, don't worry,' Xanthe said quickly. 'We'll deal with it.'

'I'll go,' Adam, one of the other stardust adults, offered.

'And me,' put in Tania, an older teenager who had been standing nearby.

Xanthe nodded and Adam and Tania flew off.

'What will they do?' Lucy asked. 'How will they stop the oil getting to the voles?'

'They're winter spirits,' Xanthe replied. 'They'll use their higher powers to clear up the pollution and make the river safe again.'

'Higher powers?' Lucy said. She glanced at her friends and saw that although Allegra was nodding, Ella and Faye were looking mystified. 'What are they, Xanthe?'

'Well, you know that the stardust that comes from your Royal Star gives you certain magical powers?' Xanthe said.

Lucy nodded. She knew that every stardust spirit's stardust came from one of the four Royal Stars – they were the brightest stars in the sky and from ancient times they had each been linked with one of the four seasons. Her star was Regulus, the summer star, and that was why she had the power to heat things up.

'Well, alongside giving you the power to either conjure fire, wind, rain or make plants grow, the stardust from your Royal Star also gives you certain higher magical powers,' Xanthe went on.

'What sort of powers?' Ella questioned.

'It depends which star your stardust comes from,' Xanthe replied. 'Winter spirits have the ability to heal and purify. Summer spirits have the ability to cast spells of protection. Spring spirits can use magical disguises and autumn spirits can read hearts and minds.'

Lucy felt a rush of excitement. She would love to know how to cast protection spells! 'How do we use our higher powers?' she asked eagerly.

'You don't yet,' Xanthe answered. 'When you can show that you have complete control of your normal magic then you will be shown how to use your higher powers.'

'But we *have* got control,' Lucy said. 'I can start a fire whenever I want.'

'You're getting much better but I think you still need to practise a little more,' Xanthe told her. 'It's not enough just to be able to start a fire, you need to be able to make it bigger or smaller at will, flaring it up or taking it down to nothing. Faye, you need to be able to control the rain in the same way, Allegra, the wind and Ella, the plants that you grow.' She smiled. 'I'm sure it won't be long before you're ready to learn about your higher powers. Now off you go and well done for alerting us about the river.'

Lucy and the others headed to the side of the clearing.

'I wonder how quickly we can get good enough,' Faye said. 'I'd love to be able to do more powerful magic.'

'Me too,' Lucy agreed.

'Well, let's get practising,' Allegra suggested. 'Lucy, why don't you and I practise over here while Ella and Faye, you practise over there?' She pointed a little way off. 'That way we don't have to stand around waiting for all four of us to have a go.'

Faye and Ella nodded in agreement.

'Can I go first?' Allegra asked as Ella and
Faye hurried off.

Lucy desperately wanted to have a go
but she nodded. 'Sure.'

Allegra held out her hands towards a
nearby pile of leaves, focusing her blue
eyes. 'Wind be with me,' she whispered.

A light breeze sprang up, swirling gently
across the grass and catching hold of a
single fallen leaf. Lucy saw Allegra frown
in concentration and then the breeze
swelled and grew stronger. The leaf rose
into the sky, twirling around in the
moonlight as it went up.

Then a second leaf was picked up and
then a third. One by one the leaves
swirled slowly upwards.

'That's brilliant!' Lucy enthused, but as she spoke Allegra lost concentration. Suddenly the breeze turned into a gust of wind and the next second the whole pile of leaves whooshed into the sky.

'Wind be gone!' Allegra said quickly. The wind ceased instantly and the leaves rained down around them.

Lucy grinned as she shook three leaves out of her hair. 'OK, that was *almost* brilliant.'

Allegra grinned back. 'You mean you didn't *want* leaves in your hair? I think it quite suits you.'

Lucy hit her playfully. 'OK, it's my turn now.' Looking up into the starry sky, she felt magic surge up from deep within her. It was the most wonderful feeling. She felt strong and in control. Every cell in her

body tingled. Stretching out her hands, she let the magic build and build. Stronger and stronger.

'Lucy?' Allegra said. 'Are you all right?'

Lucy caught the note of alarm in Allegra's voice but she ignored it.

'Fire,' she whispered, caught up in the feeling of power that surged through her, 'be with me.'

A ball of fire seemed to erupt from her fingers. It flew straight at a log and the next instant the log had burst into flames. Burning sparks shot off it and landed on the surrounding dry grass. With a crackle, the fire took hold and blazed upwards.

Lucy gasped and stepped back. She hadn't meant to set everything alight!

'Quick!' she heard Allegra cry. 'Faye, we

need rain!'

'Rain,' Faye gasped, swinging round.
'Be with –'

But even as she spoke, a raincloud had
appeared directly over the fire. In seconds
it had doused the flames. With a hiss they
died down to nothing, leaving just a thick
cloud of smoke.

Lucy felt the power drain out of her in
a rush. She stared at her friends. They were
all looking very shaky.

'That was some fire,' Allegra said.

'I–I didn't mean it to happen like that,'
Lucy stammered, feeling awful that she
had burnt such a large area. 'I didn't mean
it to be so strong. Thanks, Faye. If you
hadn't conjured that rain . . .'

'I didn't,' Faye said quickly. 'It wasn't
me.'

'It wasn't?' Lucy said.

'Lucy!'

They all turned. Xanthe was hurrying towards them with Samantha, one of the other stardust spirits. Samantha waved her hands at the cloud and commanded, 'Rain be gone.'

The raincloud disappeared. Lucy gulped. She had the definite feeling that she was in trouble. 'I–I'm sorry . . .' she started to say.

'What happened?' Xanthe asked.

'I was just trying to practise my magic,' Lucy replied. 'But the fire was much stronger than I'd meant it to be and the grass is so dry at the moment, it just got out of control. I'll be really careful next time and . . .' She saw Xanthe start to shake her head and paused.

'Lucy,' Xanthe said gently, 'I think it might be best if you didn't practise your magic for a while – at least not until the hot weather has passed.'

'Not practise?' Lucy echoed in dismay.

'No,' Xanthe replied. 'The woods are just too dry at the moment. You understand, don't you? It's just too dangerous.'

Lucy wanted to argue but she could tell there was no point. Xanthe's voice was firm. Tears prickled her eyes but Lucy blinked them back. She wasn't going to cry. She nodded and swallowed hard.

'I understand,' she whispered.

'Good.' Xanthe's eyes found Lucy's. 'You know, most young summer spirits can't start fires, Lucy,' she said softly. 'Even some of the adults find it hard. You're going to

be very powerful one day.' Lucy stared at
her. Xanthe smiled. 'The heatwave won't
last forever. You'll be able to practise again
soon enough.' With that she walked off.

Lucy looked at the others.

'Now what are we going to do?' Allegra
said in dismay.

'If Lucy can't practise, none of us
should,' Ella said loyally.

A tiny part of Lucy wanted to nod, but
she knew that would be unfair of her. 'No,
it's OK,' she said. 'You three can still
practise. I don't mind.'

'Really?' Allegra said.

'Really,' Lucy tried to sound as if she
meant it.

As Ella and Allegra walked over to the
burnt grass to try and make it grow again,
Faye looked at Lucy. 'Are you sure you're

really OK about this?' she said softly.

Lucy nodded. Faye was quieter than Ella and Allegra but she was always really sensitive to other people's feelings. 'Yeah,' she told her. 'I'm fine.'

Faye squeezed her hand. 'Well, if you're not, just say, and we won't practise.'

I'm lucky to have three such good friends, Lucy realized. *So what if I can't do magic at the moment, I can still fly and come to the woods at night.* The thought made her feel slightly less gloomy. 'Come on,' she said to Faye. 'I really am fine. Let's go and join the others.'

CHAPTER

Three

'Lucy! Breakfast!' Mrs Evans called the next morning.

Lucy yawned and blinked open her eyes.

Her mum called again from downstairs. 'Lucy!'

Lucy got out of bed and pulled on her dressing gown. Her head was aching. Usually she never felt tired after being a stardust spirit but when she'd got home

she'd been unable to get to sleep. She'd
tossed and turned in bed thinking about
what Xanthe had said. How long was it
going to be before she was allowed to
practise her magic again?

Rubbing her eyes, she went downstairs
to the kitchen. Her mum was loading the
dishwasher. 'Morning, love.'

'Morning.' Lucy yawned and sat down.

'You're looking pale,' Mrs Evans
commented. 'Are you feeling all right.'

'Fine,' Lucy replied, stifling another
yawn. 'Can I stay at Allegra's tonight?'

Mrs Evans hesitated. 'I'm not sure. You
do look tired – maybe you're coming
down with something.'

'I'm not. I'm fine,' Lucy insisted. 'Please.
We'll go to bed early.'

'I thought you said Xanthe lets you stay

up until whatever time you want.' Lucy heard the note of disapproval in her mum's voice. She had the feeling that her mum didn't really like the way Xanthe allowed Allegra to go to bed when she wanted. Or the way Allegra called her 'Xanthe' instead of Mum. Or the way there were no set meal times. Xanthe just wasn't into rules. *I wish Mum and Dad were like that,* Lucy thought enviously. She looked hopefully at her mum. 'If I promise we'll go to bed early can I stay?'

'We'll see,' Mrs Evans said. 'You have been seeing a lot of Allegra recently.'

'But she's my best friend,' Lucy said.

'I know but . . .' Mrs Evans broke off. 'Never mind. Look, I was speaking to Susan last night. How would you like to have Alison over one day next week?'

'Do I have to, Mum?' Lucy said, her heart sinking. She and Alison had known each other since they were little but Alison had changed since she'd started at her new school a year ago. She was really boastful and whenever she came over she just seemed to want to watch TV and listen to music. 'I don't like Alison.'

'Don't be silly,' her mum said briskly. 'You used to be really good friends.'

'When we were two,' Lucy said.

'Oh, Lucy,' her mum said. 'You know you'll have great fun. Now what day shall I ask her round?'

Just then the phone rang. Mrs Evans answered it. 'Hello? Oh, hello, Allegra. Yes, Lucy's here.'

Lucy took the phone, glad to have a chance to escape. 'Hi,' she said, taking the phone into the lounge.

'Hi there!' Allegra said excitedly.

'What's up?' Lucy asked.

'I've been talking to Xanthe and she said there's a way we can increase our control over our magical powers.'

'How?' Lucy asked.

'We have to use star stones.'

'What are star stones?' Lucy said.

'Come over and I'll tell you all about it.'

'OK,' Lucy said eagerly. 'See you in a few minutes.'

She hung up and hurried into the kitchen. 'Can I go round to Allegra's?'

'What? Now? But it's only nine o'clock,' her mum said.

'Please!' Lucy begged.

Her mum sighed. 'All right, finish your breakfast and then you can go. However,' she warned, 'you're to be back here by twelve. It's your turn to set the table for Sunday lunch.'

'I know,' Lucy said. 'And I'll be back, I promise.'

She gulped down the rest of her cereal, quickly washed her bowl and then ran upstairs to get dressed.

'So what do we have to do?' Lucy asked ten minutes later as she and Allegra sat down on Allegra's bed. Overhead the stars on the ceiling seemed to twinkle. Xanthe had painted the ceiling to look like the night sky.

'Well, Xanthe said that there are these things called star stones,' Allegra told her. 'The four types of stardust spirit each have a different stone. Mine is topaz because

I'm an autumn spirit, yours is onyx, Ella's
is turquoise and Faye's is amethyst.
Apparently, some stardust spirits believe
that if you wear the right star stone it
helps you control your magic.' Her eyes
shone. 'We have just *got* to try!'

'But how do we get our star stones?'
Lucy asked.

'They're just normal stones. You can buy
them at any crystal shop. There's one in
town – you know, it sells all that jewellery
and incense and stuff?'

Lucy nodded.

'Xanthe knows the owner. The crystals
and stones there aren't that expensive. We
could get necklaces, although we'd have to
be careful when we were flying that they
didn't get caught on anything . . .' Her eyes
suddenly widened. 'I know! We could get

earrings! They'd be perfect!'

'Earrings,' Lucy echoed.

Allegra nodded eagerly. 'The stones would be tiny so they wouldn't be that expensive and it would be much safer to have earrings rather than chains hanging round our necks.'

'Only one problem,' Lucy pointed out, looking enviously at Allegra's ears with their two sets of piercings. 'Faye and I don't have pierced ears.'

'So?' Allegra frowned. 'You can get them done.'

'Yeah, like my mum and dad are really going to let me,' Lucy said. She'd been wanting to have her ears pierced ever since she was seven but her mum and dad had said she had to wait until she was ten and that was almost a whole year away.

'They will. You'll just have to beg,'
Allegra said.

'It's not that easy with my mum and
dad,' Lucy protested. 'You know what
they're like.'

'They're really nice,' Allegra said. 'Look,
just tell them it's really important. They'll
understand.'

Somehow Lucy doubted it.

'No, I'm sorry, Lucy, but there's no way
I'm letting you have your ears pierced,'
Mrs Evans said firmly. She looked around
the table. 'Now, any more veggies anyone?'

Lucy was having Sunday lunch with her
family. She'd waited to ask her mum and
dad until they were sitting down and she
knew they'd be feeling relaxed. 'Please,
Mum. It's really important.'

'You can't have them done,' Rachel, Lucy's twelve-year-old sister, said, taking the carrots. 'It wouldn't be fair. Hope and I had to wait until we were ten.' She looked at their mum. 'You can't say yes, Mum.'

'Don't be mean, Rach,' Hope said. She was fourteen months older than Rachel and much nicer to Lucy. 'I think Lucy should be able to have her ears pierced. What difference does a year make?'

Lucy shot her a grateful look.

'It still wouldn't be fair,' Rachel insisted.

'Let's not have an argument about it,' their dad said calmly.

'I agree,' Mrs Evans put in. 'Sorry, Lucy, but the rule is ten years old for ear-piercing and that's the way it's staying.'

Lucy felt a growing sense of desperation. 'But Allegra's got *two* ear

piercings,' she protested. 'And she's a
month younger than me.'

'Hmmm,' Mrs Evans said, glancing at
Mr Evans. Lucy could tell from their
expressions that they didn't exactly
approve of Allegra's piercings.

'Please,' she begged.

'The answer's no, Lucy,' Mr Evans said.

Lucy felt her temper rising. It was so
unfair. Looking down at her plate, she
struggled to control herself. If she got cross

and shouted she would only end up being sent to her room.

'Could you pass the salt please, Lucy?' her dad asked.

Taking a deep breath, Lucy picked up the salt cellar and passed it down the table. If only she could make her parents realize how important it was she had her ears pierced, but she knew she couldn't. She would just have to get a necklace or a bracelet instead of earrings.

At least I won't be the only one, she tried to comfort herself, *Faye hasn't got her ears pierced either.*

An awful thought struck her. What if Faye's parents agreed to let Faye have her ears pierced?

Oh please, Lucy thought, crossing her fingers. *Please don't let me be the odd one out.*

Four

'Guess what? My mum and dad said I can have my ears pierced!' Faye's eyes shone as she landed beside Lucy, Allegra and Ella that night. 'Isn't it brilliant? I'm going to have them done tomorrow afternoon.'

Lucy's heart sank.

'How about you?' Faye asked Lucy. 'What did your parents say?'

'That I've got to wait until I'm ten,' Lucy muttered.

'Never mind,' Ella said practically. 'It's no big deal. You can get a necklace and wear your star stone that way.'

Lucy nodded, but she didn't want to wear a necklace when the others all had earrings.

'We should all meet in town tomorrow,' Allegra suggested. 'At about ten. We can go to the crystal shop together.'

'Yeah!' Ella enthused. 'I bet my dad will give us a lift into town, Faye.'

'OK,' Faye said. She looked a bit worried. 'How much money will I need, Allegra?'

'Well, I've bought earrings there for about three pounds,' Allegra said, 'but it depends on what type of stone the earrings are made out of. Some stones are more expensive than others.'

'I've got five pounds,' Faye said.

'I'm sure that will be enough,' Allegra replied. She grinned. 'I might ask Xanthe if I can have a third piercing.' She stuck out her tongue. 'Or maybe I'll have my tongue done!'

Faye and Ella giggled. Lucy smiled but it was a bit of an effort. It was so unfair that Allegra could have as many piercings as she liked and she wasn't even allowed one. 'What shall we do tonight?' she said, wanting to change the subject.

'Xanthe said to check on the voles again,' Allegra replied. 'To see that they're OK. And she said that when Adam and Tania were cleaning up the river last night they saw two otters. She wants us to build some resting places along the riverbank to encourage them to stay.'

Lucy forgot her disappointment about the earrings. 'Otters! Wow!'

Allegra grinned at her. 'What are we waiting for?'

★

On the way to the river, they played hide
and seek by camouflaging themselves.
Like all stardust spirits they had the
ability to make themselves almost
invisible by blending into whatever they
were standing near. To do it well, you
had to keep moving so that the starlight
never fell on you for too long. Lucy
loved camouflaging and she was getting
good enough to be able to almost vanish
into thin air.

'Found you!' she cried as she caught a
glimpse of Allegra, hovering near the
branches of a tree. 'And you,' she cried,
swooping down and tagging Faye, who
was blending into the background of a
bramble bush. Ella, who was the best at
camouflaging, was harder to find. Lucy
looked all around and then, hearing a

slight sound in the air, she looked up and saw a vague Ella-shape of darkness flitting across the sky. 'Got you!' she cried, soaring upwards and tagging her.

It was so much fun. *Being a stardust spirit is the best thing ever!* Lucy thought as they played the game all the way to the river.

'The water's looking cleaner,' Ella said as they flew down.

'And now the blockage has been cleared the level's gone up,' said Lucy, seeing the river was further up its banks.

'Still not high enough, though,' said Allegra. 'It won't be until it rains. We should re-cover some of the holes.'

The girls set to work covering the holes with some fresh reeds. Once the holes were hidden they moved further downstream to where the river widened out and its banks were thick with vegetation.

'This is where Adam and Tania saw the otters,' Allegra told the others. 'I asked Xanthe what we need to do and she said that otters like to have safe resting places called holts along the river. She wants us to make some out of logs and also to see if we can find some old natural holts. They're like burrows in the roots and hollowed-out trunks of trees. If we find any we've got to clear them out.'

'Well, that sounds easy enough,' Ella said. 'Why don't we get started on a log pile?'

The others nodded and set about fetching branches and logs. Starting where Adam and Tania had seen the otters, they arranged a log pile with space for the

otters to get inside and two entrance
holes.

'The holt needs to be waterproof,'
Allegra said, wiping her hands on her
silver dress. 'So we've got to make sure
there are no gaps in the roof and then
Xanthe said to disguise it by growing
plants around.'

'What type of plants?' Ella asked.

'Hawthorn, bramble, wild rose and
gorse,' Allegra replied. 'Thick prickly plants
that will keep dogs and people away.'

At last the holt was finished. Ella grew
some plants to cover the surrounding area.

'That's brilliant,' Lucy said, admiring the
gorse bushes around the holt and the roses
scrambling over the top of it. 'No one
would ever know there was an otter home
there.'

'Come on,' Allegra said. 'This pile of logs is fine now. Let's go and see if we can find any natural holts.'

They flew down the river. 'That looks like it could be a natural one!' Ella said, pointing to an old tree on the riverbank with a hollowed-out trunk.

They swooped down. The hollow was overgrown with a mat of plants, however it looked like it was just the sort of place that an otter might use for a den. They cleared it out, removing the mouldy leaves and replacing them with some clean dry ones.

'I hope the otters do come here,' Ella said.

'Yeah, it would be brilliant,' Allegra agreed. 'We could watch them and maybe they'd have babies. Baby otters are so cute!'

'We'll have to come back every night and check,' Faye said.

Lucy looked down the river. 'Maybe there are some more holts further on that we could clear out.'

They flew on. By the end of that night they had cleared out three holts and constructed two more log piles.

'All we need now are some otters,' Ella said.

Feeling tired but happy, Lucy looked up at the sky. The constellation of Orion the hunter could just be seen appearing in the east, which meant it was about three o'clock in the morning. 'We should be getting home,' she said. She always liked to be back well before dawn just in case her mum or dad decided to get up early.

Allegra nodded. 'I'll see you at mine

tomorrow morning, Luce. Xanthe will take us into town.'

Lucy had almost forgotten about the shopping trip the next day. As she remembered, the happiness she'd been feeling slowly faded away.

'I can't wait to get our star stones,' Ella said.

'Yeah, it's going to be so cool,' Faye agreed.

Looking round at the others' excited faces, Lucy tried to summon up some enthusiasm but it was hard. She really wanted her own star stone, but she didn't want a necklace when they all had earrings.

'Come on then, Faye,' Ella said. 'See you tomorrow!'

She and Ella flew off and Lucy and

Allegra headed home.

'I wonder what it will be like to do magic with our star stones,' Allegra said as they weaved in and out of the trees. 'Do you think it will be loads easier?'

Lucy shrugged.

'I bet you'll be brilliant at controlling your magic when you've got yours,' Allegra told her.

Lucy sighed as she remembered another thing to be fed up about. 'Well I'm not going to be able to practise, am I? You know what your mum said. I'm not allowed to do any magic until the weather breaks.'

'We could always find a quiet bit of the woods where you could practise,' Allegra said. 'Faye could put out any fires that you make.'

'I guess.' Lucy felt suddenly hopeful. Maybe Allegra was right. Perhaps, once she got her star stone, she could practise in secret until she got really good – then she could show Xanthe and the other stardust spirits and they'd have to let her start doing her magic again. Maybe she'd even be so good that they would let her learn about her higher powers. Lucy imagined herself swooping around the clearing, effortlessly starting fires and putting them out while the older spirits watched admiringly.

A grin spread across her face. OK, so maybe getting her star stone *was* going to be exciting after all!

Five

At nine forty the next morning, Lucy
went to Allegra's house. She had five
pounds in her purse. She hoped it would
be enough to buy a necklace.

Allegra was ready and waiting when she
arrived. She opened the door as Lucy
walked up the overgrown path. 'Hi!' she
called. 'Xanthe's just coming, let's get into
the car.'

Ten minutes later they were heading towards town. It was another hot day and, seeing the sun blazing down out of the clear blue sky, Lucy was glad she was wearing shorts.

'I can't wait to get to the shop,' Allegra enthused as they drove into town. 'I so want to see my star stone. It's going to be brilliant doing magic with it.'

Xanthe glanced over her shoulder. 'Don't build star stones up to be more than they are, Allegra,' she said. 'I know some stardust spirits believe that star stones can help control stardust magic, but proper control over your magic comes from your mind and not from a stone.'

'What do you mean?' Allegra asked.

'To control your magic you need to concentrate your thoughts and believe in what you are doing,' Xanthe said. 'Star stones can help because they give you something to focus on. But they don't work miracles.'

'Well, I bet we'll be loads better at controlling our magic when we've got them,' Allegra said, looking at Lucy, who nodded in agreement.

Xanthe smiled at them. 'Well, I guess as long as you believe that, that's all that matters.'

Lucy wondered what Xanthe meant but she didn't have time to puzzle about it. Xanthe parked the car and they got out.

Ella and Faye were waiting by the fountain in the town square. 'Dad's gone to HMV,' Ella explained. 'He's meeting us back here in half an hour.'

'Let's go to the crystal shop then,'
Allegra said.

She and Xanthe led the way out of the
main square and down a side road. They
turned into a narrow street and then Lucy
saw the shop. It was next to a rather scary-
looking place that did tattoos and
piercings. Lucy looked in the crystal shop's
window. Brightly patterned materials were
draped over boxes and on the boxes were
wooden trays of crystals, rings, bangles and
necklaces, incense burners and scented
candles. A sign over the window read
Taryn's Crystals and Hand-made Jewellery.

The door was open and silver wind
chimes were hanging in the doorway. As
they went in the chimes tinkled merrily.
The shop was quite dark and cool inside
and a woman was sitting behind the

counter wearing a fringed skirt in different
shades of green. Her long red hair was
piled up on her head. 'Hello, Xanthe,' she
smiled. 'What can I do for you today?'

'Allegra and her friends would like to
look at some of your crystals, Taryn,'
Xanthe replied.

'We want to buy earrings,' Allegra put in.

'They each want earrings with different
types of crystal,' Xanthe said. 'Allegra's after
topaz, Ella wants turquoise, Faye wants
amethyst and Lucy wants onyx.' A look
passed between her and Taryn and Lucy
wondered whether Taryn was a stardust
spirit too.

'Well, the earrings are right here,' Taryn
told them, pointing to a large velvet
display board studded with numerous pairs
of earrings, each with different crystal

centres. 'Have a look. All the crystals are labelled.'

Allegra, Ella and Faye crowded round the board. Lucy hung back. 'Don't you want to see, Lucy?' Xanthe said to her.

'I'm not allowed to have my ears pierced,' Lucy admitted, glancing around the shop. 'I was going to look for a necklace.'

'The necklaces are just over there,' Taryn said, pointing to a display case on the back wall of the shop. Silver chains hung from tiny nails, each with a crystal hanging from it. 'What stone was it that you wanted?'

'Onyx,' Lucy replied eagerly.

'Ah.' Taryn frowned. 'Well, I haven't got much in and the pieces I do have are quite expensive.'

Lucy's heart dropped. 'Oh.'

'There's this necklace.' Taryn held out a beautiful silver necklace with an oval pendant. Lucy stared. The polished stone was striped in fine lines of black and white. For a moment she felt a flicker of disappointment. She'd been hoping for a purple stone, or maybe blue. But then, as she looked at the stone, she felt something strange happen inside her. The stone seemed to gleam and glow in the shop's light. Suddenly she wanted to touch it . . .

Taryn seemed to read her thoughts. 'Here,' she offered, holding the pendant out. Lucy held the necklace in her cupped hands. The stone felt warm and smooth. 'It's beautiful,' Lucy whispered and then she saw the price tag: *twenty pounds*. Feeling a stab of disappointment, Lucy made herself give the necklace back to

Taryn. 'I'm sorry. It's too expensive. Have you got anything cheaper?'

'There are some onyx earrings that are five pounds but they're not going to be much good if you haven't got pierced ears.' Taryn held out a pair of earrings. The stones were shaped into two circles of glowing black striped with white. They were tiny but perfect. Lucy desperately wanted them but she had to shake her head. 'I wouldn't be able to wear them.'

'Well, I'm afraid that's all the onyx jewellery I've got at the moment,' Taryn said. 'I should be getting some more supplies in about six weeks' time. If I get some onyx I could make you up a necklace with a small pendant then. Would you like me to do that?'

Lucy nodded but inwardly she was dismayed. Six weeks! That was ages. 'Thank you,' she muttered. She turned away and pretended to be looking at a display of essential oils so that no one could see how upset she was.

'These earrings are perfect!' she heard Allegra exclaim. 'Look how the stones twinkle.'

'I want these ones,' Ella said.

'And I like these,' Faye put in.

Soon the cash till was ringing up their purchases. Clutching a paper bag each, Allegra, Ella and Faye crowded out of the shop with Lucy trailing behind.

'Look!' Allegra said, taking her earrings out of the bag and holding them up to the light. They twinkled pale gold.

'I'm going to put mine in as soon as I

get home,' said Ella, taking hers out of
their bag as well. They were little ovals of
sky-blue.

'I wish you'd been able to get
something,' Faye said, looking at Lucy
with concern.

Lucy tried to shrug. 'I'll get something
soon.'

'Six weeks isn't soon,' Ella blurted out.

'Ella's right,' Allegra said. She turned to
Xanthe. 'Can't we go to another shop,
Mum?'

'There isn't another crystal shop in
town,' Xanthe replied.

'I'll wait,' Lucy said, swallowing hard.
'It doesn't matter.'

'Couldn't you buy the earrings and just
hold them?' Faye suggested.

Allegra shook her head. 'That wouldn't

be any good. You have to actually wear your star stones, don't you, Mum?'

Xanthe nodded. 'That's what people seem to believe.' She studied Lucy's downcast face for a moment then spoke briskly. 'Come on. I'll treat you all to an ice cream.'

By the time Lucy got home later that morning, she was feeling really miserable. The others had tried not to talk about their earrings much, but she could tell they were really thrilled at the thought of trying out their magic that night. And Faye had been bursting with excitement about getting her ears pierced that afternoon.

'Are you staying for lunch?' Allegra asked as they got out of the car.

Lucy shook her head. 'Mum wants me
to go home.'

'OK, see you this evening,' Allegra said.

'Yeah, see you,' Lucy said, trying to
force a smile. 'Thanks for the lift, Xanthe.'

'No problem. See you later,' Xanthe
said.

Lucy walked up the driveway. The sun
was beating down and she felt hot and fed
up. First she'd been banned from practising
her magic and now she couldn't even have
her star stone like the others. It was so
unfair. Why couldn't she have her ears
pierced like everyone else? Then she could
have bought the earrings.

She kicked a pebble crossly. Her hair
was sticking to the back of her neck and
her canvas shoes were rubbing.

'Hi!' Mrs Evans said cheerfully as Lucy

stomped into the kitchen. 'Did you have a good shopping trip?'

'No,' Lucy muttered. She pulled off her shoes and sat down.

'Is something the matter?' Mrs Evans asked.

'No.' Lucy replied but then anger seemed to boil up inside her and the words burst out of her. 'Yes, everything! It's not fair, Mum. Why *can't* I have my ears pierced?'

The concern left Mrs Evans' face. 'Let's not start this again,' she sighed. 'The answer's no.'

'But it's so unfair!' Lucy said again. 'Everyone else has pierced ears!'

Mrs Evans looked sceptical. 'By everyone you mean Allegra.'

'Not just her, El–' Lucy stopped herself

just in time. It was always hard to
remember that her mum didn't know Ella
and Faye. 'Everyone at school has them
done. I've got to have them too!'

'I hardly think you've *got* to,' Mrs Evans
said drily. She shook her head. 'Look, I
know it seems important, love, but Dad
and I really don't want you to have them
done until you're ten. It's only eight
months away. It's not that long to wait.'

Lucy banged the table. 'It is! You *don't*
understand! I need them done now!'

Mrs Evans frowned. 'Lucy! I won't have
you talking to me in that tone of voice.
Now start being sensible or you can go to
your bedroom.'

Lucy glared at her. 'I'll go to my room
then.' She knew she was behaving badly but
she didn't care. She walked to the door.

'Fine,' Mrs Evans said firmly. 'Maybe when you come down you'll be in a better mood. And while you're up there, can you please tidy up? I spoke to Susan this morning and Alison's coming round to spend the day with you tomorrow.'

It was the last straw. 'Oh, great,' Lucy groaned at the thought of spending the day with boring Alison. 'Just great!'

CHAPTER

Six

'Look! Watch this!' Allegra exclaimed.

The breeze that Allegra had just
conjured swirled a single leaf into the air
before growing stronger and stronger,
picking up more and more leaves until
there was a twirling cloud of them. Then
the breeze died down and the leaves
floated to the floor until there was only a
single leaf left.

'Wind be gone,' Allegra whispered as the last leaf drifted to the ground.

'That was fantastic!' Ella cried.

Faye nodded. 'I've never seen you have so much control.'

'The star stones make such a difference!'
Allegra said, her eyes shining. 'I just
concentrated on them and suddenly I
knew I could control the wind. It was an
amazing feeling. You try, Ella.'

Lucy watched as Ella touched her hand
to her earrings and focused on a patch on
the ground. A little forget-me-not grew up,
its tiny sky-blue flower head bobbing up
and down. And then another and another
until there were six round patches of them
on the floor of the clearing.

'Cool!' Allegra said. 'It's so easy with the
star stones, isn't it?'

'Yeah,' Ella said, grinning. She caught
sight of Lucy's face and looked suddenly
guilty. 'I wish you had your star stone too,
Lucy.'

Lucy nodded. She hated not being able

to do anything. The others started practising again.

'Lucy.'

Lucy looked round. Xanthe was walking over to her. 'It must be hard just watching. Would you like to practise too?'

'But I thought you said I couldn't because of the weather,' Lucy said. 'And anyway, I haven't got my star stone.'

'There's enough of us here to deal with a fire if it gets out of control,' Xanthe said glancing around the clearing where the older stardust spirits were exchanging news. 'And as for your star stone, well, you don't need that. Controlling your magic is all down to you – you just need to concentrate and believe that you can. Come on, let's have a try.'

Lucy followed Xanthe and knelt on the ground.

'Now let's see if you can start a small fire and then take it right down to being just a smouldering log,' Xanthe suggested. 'Breathe in first. You need to be feeling calm and in control.'

Lucy took a deep breath. Starlight fell on her bare arms, making them shimmer. She stared at a fallen branch.

'Just believe you can do it,' Xanthe told her softly.

Lucy stretched out her hands. 'Fire, be with me,' she breathed.

Power started to surge through her, hot and tingling. She felt it build but this time she didn't let it get too strong. *Small fire, small fire*, she thought, concentrating hard. The fallen branch burst into flame. Lucy stared at the flickering, crackling fire. It wasn't getting any bigger. *I can do this*, she realized. *I can control it.*

'Make it get smaller,' Xanthe prompted her.

Shrink, Lucy thought. The fire began to die down. It was hard and took a lot of effort.

If I had my star stone I bet this would be easier. The thought crossed Lucy's mind before she knew it.

The flames flared upwards. Frustration filled Lucy. *I can't do this*, she thought. *I need my star stone. I can't do it on my own.*

Whoosh! The fire shot up in a towering column. Lucy gasped in alarm as the fire flickered at the branches of the oak tree.

A second later a raincloud had appeared and rain was pouring down on the fire, dousing it until all that was left was a burnt and soggy circle of grass.

'I'm sorry,' Lucy stammered.

'It's OK,' Xanthe said quickly. 'Wind be with me,' she whispered. As the wind swirled round, carrying away the smoke, Xanthe put a hand on Lucy's shoulder. 'Maybe letting you practise wasn't such a good idea after all,' she said ruefully.

'If I had my star stone I could control it!' Lucy burst out. 'I —'

'No,' Xanthe interrupted. 'Lucy,' she said gently, 'I've already told you. The star stones don't work miracles. You need to find the control inside yourself.' She sighed. 'Don't worry about it. You'll get there in the end.'

But when? Lucy wanted to shout.

★

83

When Lucy finally flew home that evening, she kept thinking about how good the others were becoming at controlling their magic powers. What if they got to learn about their higher powers and she didn't? It would be awful. She tossed and turned in her bed. It didn't help that in the morning she would be faced with the prospect of putting up with Alison all day.

'Mum,' she asked the next morning, 'can Allegra come over this morning?'

'No, not today,' Mrs Evans replied. 'You know Alison's coming.'

'But can't Allegra come round too?' Lucy said.

Mrs Evans shook her head.

'Why?' Lucy asked, frowning.

'You don't have to see Allegra every day,' Mrs Evans said.

'You don't like Allegra, do you?' Lucy said quickly.

'Of course I do,' Mrs Evans replied. 'It's just that, well . . .' she hesitated. 'Allegra and Xanthe have a very different lifestyle from ours and I've noticed a change in you since you started being friends with Allegra.'

'I haven't changed!' Lucy protested.

'You have. All this business about having your ears pierced. You never used to worry about things like that. I think maybe you and Allegra spend too much time together.'

'We don't!' Lucy exclaimed in alarm.

Just then there was the sound of a car on the driveway.

'Let's not get into this now,' Mrs Evans said. 'Can you go and let Alison in please?'

Lucy went to the door, feeling shocked. She couldn't believe her mum thought she spent too much time with Allegra.

'Hi,' Alison muttered, coming up the path with her mum. She was tall and pretty with dark, shoulder-length hair, but her face had a sulky expression.

'Hi,' Lucy said back.

They went through into the kitchen. After Susan, Alison's mum, had chatted for a while, she left. Mrs Evans got out some biscuits and orange squash. 'So are you having a good summer holiday, Alison?' she asked.

Alison nodded.

'And are you going anywhere nice?'

'America,' Alison replied briefly.

'How exciting,' Mrs Evans smiled.

'I've been three times before,' Alison said, sounding bored.

Mrs Evans handed her a glass of squash. 'Still, I'm sure you'll have a great time.'

Alison just shrugged and didn't even say thank you for the drink. 'I don't like those biscuits,' she said looking at the packet. 'They're just economy ones.'

Lucy saw her mum's face tighten. 'Well, I'm afraid we haven't got any others,' Mrs Evans said briskly.

Alison sighed and took one, then she and Lucy went upstairs.

'Your bedroom's still pink,' Alison said, raising her eyebrows. 'Don't you think that's a bit babyish, Lucy?'

Lucy shrugged. She liked her bedroom. The walls were a deep dusky rose colour and she had lilac curtains with fairies on.

'My room's black and white now,'
Alison informed her. She looked around.
'I can't believe you still haven't got a TV
in your room. I've got a TV, a DVD player
and a computer.' Alison went to the
window. 'So what are we going to do
today?' she said sounding bored.

'I don't know,' Lucy replied.

'Can we watch telly?'

Lucy nodded. 'Yes.' Somehow she had
the feeling it was going to be a very long
day.

She was right. The hours dragged by until
teatime. All Alison wanted to do was to
watch TV and then when Mrs Evans told
them they had to turn it off Alison said
she wanted to sunbathe in the garden.

While they sat in the garden she boasted about the amazing new house she and her parents had just moved to which had a swimming pool.

Lucy got so bored, she ended up going off and playing with Thumper in the shade of the greenhouse. As she fed him pieces of carrot, she looked longingly at the wall that separated her garden from Allegra's. She would be having so much more fun if Allegra was with her instead of Alison.

By teatime, Lucy began to get the impression that her mum was getting distinctly fed up with Alison too. She kept suggesting all sorts of things they might like to do, like getting the old paddling pool out or the giant snakes and ladders game, but Alison just kept saying she was bored. By four o'clock, Mrs Evans gave up

and told them they could watch TV until
Susan came.

The two girls sat in silence at opposite
ends of the sofa. Lucy thought about the
night ahead and wished she could just
turn herself into a stardust spirit there and
then. Anything to escape from Alison.

Newsround came on the TV. There was
a report on forest fires. Lucy began to
listen. The reporter said that the hot
weather was leading to a spate of forest
fires across the south-west. Then there
were pictures of firefighters tackling the
blazes on Dartmoor.

'This is boring, let's turn over,' Alison
said, reaching for the remote control.

'No, wait a minute,' Lucy said. She
watched the fires on the screen spreading
rapidly, burning the dried grass and trees.
It reminded her of the night before. In
dry conditions fires could spread so
quickly.

'To stop the blazes, firefighters are
creating firebreaks,' the reporter
explained. 'The idea is that they use
carefully controlled fires to burn away

the vegetation before the forest fire can reach it. When it reaches the firebreak, there is nothing left to burn up and it can finally be put out.'

'Boring!' Alison said. She pressed the remote control and the channel changed.

Lucy glowered at her. She'd thought the piece about forest fires had been really interesting. And worrying. What if a fire started in the woods? It was a troubling thought.

'Alison! Lucy!' Mrs Evans shouted, sounding relieved. 'Susan's here.'

Alison got her things and went to meet her mum at the front door. Lucy noted that her mum didn't press any invitations on her to come back. 'We'll see you soon,' she said brightly.

'Yes, Lucy must come and visit us for

the day,' Susan said. 'Maybe next week.'

'Maybe,' Mrs Evans said non-committally.

As soon as Susan and Alison drove off, Mrs Evans shut the door and sighed with relief. 'Goodness! That was hard work.' She shook her head. 'I'm sorry, love. You were right. You and Alison really don't have anything in common any more.'

'So I don't have to have her round again?' Lucy asked eagerly.

'No,' her mum replied. 'You don't.' She smiled. 'I'm really pleased you behaved so well today even though Alison was so difficult. So how about, as a special treat, you and I go into town together tomorrow morning. We can do whatever you want.'

'OK,' Lucy looked hopefully at her. 'Can I have my ears pierced?'

Mrs Evans raised her eyebrows. 'Nice try, Lucy, but I think you know the answer to that.'

CHAPTER

Seven

'I believe in stardust,' Lucy whispered as
she stood by her window sill that night.
Her skin tingled. Her body felt as if it was
getting lighter and lighter. 'I believe in
stardust. I believe in stardust!'

As she spoke the final word, she rose,
swirling around in the air as her body
changed into pure stardust and her
pyjamas turned into a shimmering gold

dress. Excitement raced through her. It didn't matter how many times she turned into a stardust spirit, the transformation was always thrilling.

Flying over the shadowy garden towards Allegra's house, Lucy wondered what they were going to do that evening. Her heart sank slightly as she realized that Allegra, Faye and Ella were sure to want to practise their magic again.

I don't have to watch, she thought. *I can always go and do something else.* But she knew she wouldn't. She would hate the others to think she was upset or, even worse, sulking because she couldn't join in.

'Hi,' Allegra said, flying out to meet her.

'What's up?' Lucy asked, seeing a worried frown on Allegra's face.

'Nothing,' Allegra said quickly. 'Come on, let's go.'

They flew towards the woods. Allegra didn't say a word.

Lucy could tell something was bothering her. 'OK,' she said as they reached the trees. 'Something's the matter. What is it?'

Allegra hesitated. 'There's going to be a stardust feast tomorrow night. There'll be food and dancing and stuff.'

'Cool.' Lucy couldn't understand why Allegra looked so worried. 'Isn't it?'

'Yeah.' Allegra bit her lower lip. 'It's just, well, Xanthe said that Faye, Ella and I can show the other stardust spirits how good we are at using our magical powers at the feast. If we control our magic well, then they'll let us start learning about our higher powers.'

Lucy stared at Allegra. 'But what about me?'

Allegra looked very uncomfortable. 'Mum says you'll have to wait to show your magic until the heatwave passes.'

Lucy felt as if her stomach had just plunged down a lift shaft. Allegra and the others were going to get to learn about their higher powers and she wasn't.

'Are — are you OK, Luce?' Allegra asked.

'Yeah,' Lucy muttered. But she wasn't. She couldn't bear it. She just couldn't bear it.

'If you had your star stone I'm sure you'd be able to control your magic really well, even though it's so dry,' Allegra said quickly. 'Look, can't you borrow some money off your parents and buy that necklace? Then you could show Xanthe how good you are at controlling your magic and maybe she'd let you join in at the feast too.'

Lucy shook her head. 'There's no way Mum and Dad would let me spend twenty pounds on a necklace,' she said dully. She thought of the earrings. 'Oh, if only I had my ears pierced! Why did it have to be *only* a necklace or earrings? Why not a ring or a bracelet?' She scowled at her bad luck.

Allegra stared at her as if she'd suddenly had an idea.

'What?' Lucy said.

Allegra shook her head. 'Nothing.' But her eyes were sparkling with excitement.

'What is it?' Lucy said.

But Allegra wouldn't say anything more.

They reached the clearing. Faye and
Ella were already there. 'Hi!' Ella called.
'Have you heard about this feast?'

'Yeah. Xanthe told me,' Allegra replied.

'I'll . . . um . . . go and find out what
we're doing tonight,' Lucy said hastily. The
last thing she wanted was to listen to Ella,
Allegra and Faye talking about the feast
and showing off their magic powers. She
flew swiftly away to where Xanthe was
talking to Tania. While Lucy waited for the
conversation to finish, she glanced back at
the others. They were whispering together
and they kept looking in her direction.

Lucy swallowed and turned away. She
was sure they were talking about how they
were going to be able to prove they were
ready to learn about their higher powers –
and how she wasn't.

I don't care, she thought fiercely. *I really don't.*

But she did. She could hardly think of anything else. Even when she and the others went to check on the otter holts and she saw two otters swimming in the river, she was only delighted for a few moments before she remembered the feast again.

It didn't help that Allegra, Ella and Faye kept whispering to each other whenever they thought she wasn't looking.

In the end, Lucy couldn't take it any longer. 'I'm going home,' she said.

'Already?' Allegra said.

Lucy nodded. 'I'm not feeling well,' she lied. 'Look, I'll see you tomorrow.'

'But Lucy –' Faye began.

'Bye,' Lucy interrupted and she flew away.

As she reached the edge of the trees, she looked back and saw Allegra, Faye and Ella talking to each other again. They looked eager and excited.

Lucy's stomach clenched. She imagined what it was going to be like when they could use their higher powers and she couldn't. She'd be the odd one out.

No, she thought. *I can't let it happen.*

But what could she do? She searched for a solution. If only she could buy her star stones. But how *could* she? She couldn't afford the necklace and she didn't have pierced ears.

I could have them pierced.

She thought about her mum and dad. They would go mad.

But what could they really do? They could shout at her but that wouldn't go on forever. They could stop her pocket money but that didn't matter. They could ground her. But she'd still be able to get out at night and see Allegra.

They'd be really upset.

Lucy quickly pushed that thought away.

I'll do it, she decided, feeling a rush of fear and excitement. *I'll go and have my ears pierced tomorrow!*

Eight

'Mum, can Allegra come into town with us?' Lucy asked at breakfast.

Mrs Evans hesitated.

'Please,' Lucy begged. She needed Allegra to come. Her mum would never let her go off on her own in town, and also she didn't want to go into the ear-piercing shop by herself.

'All right,' Mrs Evans agreed. 'I suppose

this *is* supposed to be your treat.'

Lucy hurried to the phone and punched in Allegra's number. 'Hi, it's me,' she said when Allegra answered. 'Can you come into town with me this morning? Mum's said she'll give us a lift.'

'Well, I was supposed to be going out with Xanthe,' Allegra said.

'Please. I really need you to come.' Lucy didn't dare say anything else while her mum was nearby.

'OK,' Allegra agreed.

'Great!' Lucy said, relieved. 'Come round in about half an hour.'

Lucy could hardly sit still on the drive into town. It was very hard to pretend it was just an ordinary shopping trip. Luckily her mum and Allegra didn't seem to notice.

'Are you enjoying the summer holidays, Allegra?' Mrs Evans asked politely.

'Yes,' Allegra smiled. 'It's really nice not being at school. Xanthe and I are going to build a pond in our garden this summer.'

'That sounds interesting,' Mrs Evans replied.

Allegra nodded. 'We're going to have a rockery and fish, and plant it with all sorts of wild flowers. I want to plant purple loosestrife and great willowherb around it. They love damp areas and they'll attract bees and butterflies. I'd also like to have some water lilies.'

Mrs Evans glanced round at her. 'You seem to know a lot about plants.'

'Xanthe and I love gardening,' Allegra said happily. 'It's really fun. You'll have to

come and see our pond when it's finished,
Mrs Evans.'

'I'd like that.' Mrs Evans smiled and
Lucy got the distinct impression that her
mum was comparing Allegra very
favourably with Alison from the day
before. 'Now, what would you two like to
do in town? I need to call in at the bank
and get a birthday present for a work
friend, but apart from that we can do
whatever you want.'

Lucy's heart started to beat faster. 'Um
. . . could Allegra and I go off on our own
while you're shopping?' she asked. 'We
could meet up at Gino's café?'

'OK,' Mrs Evans agreed.

The bank was near to the street
where Taryn's shop and the ear-piercing
place were. 'I'll see you at Gino's in half

an hour,' Mrs Evans said as she
left them.

'So what shall we do?' Allegra said,
looking around. 'We could go to –'

'I want to go to the ear-piercing place
next to Taryn's shop,' Lucy interrupted.
'I'm going to have my ears pierced.' She
grinned nervously.

'You're what?' Allegra stared at her as if
she'd gone mad. 'But what about your
mum and dad?'

'What about them?' Lucy said. She
stuck her chin up defiantly and tried to
ignore the now frantic banging of her
heart. 'I'm going to have my ears pierced
and that's that. Come on, let's go!' She
started to walk along the street.

Allegra hurried after her. 'Lucy, stop!
You can't have your ears pierced.'

Lucy frowned. 'Why not?'

'Your mum and dad will go mad!'

'I don't care,' Lucy said, breaking into a
run.

Allegra caught her by the door of the
shop. 'Lucy!' she gasped, grabbing her arm.
'Please don't. Your mum will be so upset.'

Lucy couldn't believe Allegra was trying
to stop her. 'I thought you'd be pleased. I
thought you'd want me to have my ears
done.'

'I do, but not if your parents have said
you can't.' Allegra exclaimed. 'They'll never
trust you again. It's not worth it, Lucy.'

Lucy's mind whirled in confusion. She'd
been sure Allegra would back her up and
tell her that she was doing the right thing.
She hesitated, her hand on the door handle.

'I know you want your ears done so

you can have your star stones,' Allegra said, 'but you don't have to. Listen, it's supposed to be a surprise but –'

'Lucy!'

Lucy and Allegra swung round. Mrs Evans was coming down the street. It was clear she had seen Lucy with her hand on the door of the ear-piercing shop. 'Lucy!' she exclaimed. 'Whatever do you think you're doing?'

'I'm not doing anything,' Lucy said, feeling a blush spread from her toes all the way up her body. People in the street were looking at her.

Mrs Evans hurried towards them. 'Were you about to about to go and get your ears pierced?'

Lucy felt sick. She was in such deep trouble. 'No!'

It was clear her mum didn't believe her. 'Lucy, you know how Dad and I feel about the subject. I can't believe you could be so deceitful as to plan to do it behind our backs.' Mrs Evans swung round to Allegra. 'Have you been encouraging her, Allegra?'

'No,' Allegra gasped.

'Allegra didn't have anything to do with it!' Lucy said quickly. More and more people were looking. 'She was trying to stop me!'

Mrs Evans obviously thought it was all Allegra's idea. 'I'll be speaking to your mother when we get home,' she said angrily to her.

'No, Mum!' Lucy burst out. 'It's not Allegra's fault!'

'I don't want to hear another word from you,' Mrs Evans said, shaking her

head. 'I am *so* disappointed in you, Lucy.
I really am.'

Looking at her mum's face with its
mixture of anger and worry, Lucy
suddenly couldn't bear it any longer. A sob
burst out of her and, turning, she ran off
down the street.

'Lucy!' her mum cried.

Lucy ignored her. Tears streaked from
her eyes. Everything had gone wrong. She
reached the end of the street. She just
wanted to run away.

She heard footsteps catching up with
her and the next second, Allegra was
grabbing her arm. 'Wait!'

Lucy tried to pull away.

'Don't run away, you'll make it worse,'
Allegra gasped. 'You need to talk to your
mum.'

Lucy hesitated but, deep down, she knew Allegra was right. Mrs Evans came running up. Lucy braced herself to be shouted at again but her mum just looked very relieved that she had stopped.

'Oh, Lucy, sweetheart,' she said, looking very shaky. 'I thought you were going to run off into town on your own. I'm sorry I shouted at you. I was just really shaken when I saw you about to go into that place.' She hugged Lucy tight. 'Come on, I think we need to talk. Let's sit down over there.'

They walked over to a nearby bench and sat down. Lucy stared at her knees.

Mrs Evans sighed. 'Whatever possessed you to think about having your ears done in secret, Lucy?'

'I . . . I don't know,' Lucy said in a small voice. 'I just want them done.' She looked at Allegra. 'It's important, isn't it, Allegra?'

To her surprise, Allegra shook her head. 'It's not that important, Luce,' she said seriously. 'It would have been wrong to have your ears done when your mum and dad didn't want you to.' She looked at Mrs Evans. 'I really wasn't trying to make Lucy have her ears pierced, Mrs Evans. I *was* trying to stop her.'

Lucy nodded. 'She was, Mum.'

Mrs Evans rubbed her forehead. 'I owe you an apology then, Allegra. I'm very sorry. I should never have accused you of encouraging Lucy and thank you for trying to stop her. You've been a good friend.'

'I just know how upset my mum would be if I went and had my ears pierced without telling her. She'd find it hard to trust me ever again.'

Mrs Evans looked at Lucy. 'Allegra's right,' she said. 'Dad and I would have felt really let down if you'd had your ears pierced behind our backs. We want you to wait until you're ten before having them done. We both believe that sometimes it's better to wait for things you really want.'

Lucy looked at her knees.

Mrs Evans squeezed her hand. 'Oh, Lucy,' she sighed. 'I know we probably seem horribly strict to you but it's only because we love you. Do you understand that? We really do love you.'

'I know,' Lucy whispered.

Her mum put her arms around her and all at once Lucy knew she did understand – she really did. Hugging her mum back she felt a weight slip off her shoulders. She

didn't want to argue with her parents. She
wanted them to be pleased with her and
she was glad she hadn't had her ears done,
even if it did mean she was different from
Allegra, Ella and Faye. 'I love you too,
Mum,' she said, hugging her hard.

As they separated, Mrs Evans smiled.
'Well,' she said, 'I had planned that this

shopping trip was going to be fun so how about I get us all an ice cream and then we go and buy some supplies so you two can have an extra special sleepover tomorrow evening?'

'Cool!' Allegra exclaimed.

Lucy nodded. 'That sounds great!'

'OK, then,' Mrs Evans declared. 'Let's start with the ice cream. How about a ninety-nine each with strawberry sauce?'

'Yes please!' Allegra and Lucy replied in unison.

Lucy watched her mum walk over to the ice-cream van. She had a feeling that her mum wasn't going to say anything about her spending too much time with Allegra in the future.

Allegra looked at her. 'You know, having your ears pierced is really not that important, Luce.'

Lucy turned to her. 'It's easy for you to say. You've got your ears pierced. You're not the odd one out.'

'Neither are you,' Allegra protested.

Lucy hesitated and then decided to say what she was feeling. 'I felt like it last night,' she admitted. 'When you three were going off together.'

'Going off!' Allegra stared at her. 'What do you mean?'

Lucy bit her lip. 'I saw you whispering together.'

'Whispering? Lucy!' Allegra exclaimed. 'We weren't going off. We were planning a surprise – for you.'

Lucy was completely taken aback. 'What sort of surprise?'

'I can't tell you,' Allegra replied. 'It's

supposed to be a secret and Faye and Ella would kill me. But I absolutely swear we haven't been going off together.'

'Oh.' Lucy suddenly started to feel much better. 'Oh, right. I thought maybe because I didn't have my star stone . . .'

Allegra looked at her in astonishment. 'As if we'd go off and leave you out because of that. We're your friends!'

'Really?' Lucy said anxiously.

'Really!' Allegra shook her head and sighed in exasperation. 'You know, you can be a bit of an idiot sometimes, Lucy Evans.'

Lucy grinned, feeling very happy for the first time in days. 'I guess I can.'

CHAPTER

Nine

Lucy's dad decided to watch a film that night. It went on late and Lucy waited impatiently for him to go to bed. She was longing to get to the stardust glade to find out what her surprise was. At long last, he came upstairs and soon the house fell silent. Quickly turning into a stardust spirit, Lucy flew out through the window. She didn't want to miss the start of the feast!

Feeling happier than she had done in a long time, she swooped through the sky and into the woods. *The drought won't last forever*, she thought. *As soon as it's over I'll be able to start practising again and then I'll show I'm ready to learn about my higher powers too and Allegra, Ella, Faye and I can learn together . . .*

Just then a familiar smell tingled in her nostrils. *Smoke.* Alarm flickered through her. Where was it coming from? She flew up above the trees. There! A short distance away a spiral of pale grey smoke was rising up into the night sky.

She flew towards it. A thicket of bramble bushes was on fire. Lucy saw a blackened patch of grass where someone had obviously been having a campfire. It had been put out, but not well enough.

The flames were burning up the dry leaves and branches and beginning to lick the trunks of the nearby trees.

Lucy's heart raced. If the fire wasn't stopped, it would spread rapidly. She had to get help! A gust of wind sent smoke billowing around her. Coughing and spluttering, she flew upwards. Below her, the crackling of the fire was building into a roar.

'Help!' Lucy yelled. 'Someone! Help!'

But even as she shouted, she knew it was useless. The other stardust spirits would all be getting ready for the feast. What could she do? Flying to the glade and coming back with help would take ages. The fire could cause so much damage by then.

Reaching clear sky, she looked down,

her eyes stinging from the smoke. Birds
were flying upwards and squirrels were
jumping from tree to tree as they fled
from the flames. Their nests and homes
would be destroyed, but they were the
lucky ones. At least they could escape.
Lucy thought of the animals who lived in
the undergrowth – the rabbits, the mice,
the shrews, the voles. How many of them

were trapped down there?

Lucy dodged a burning leaf. *If only I could make rain*, she thought frantically. *But all I can do is make fire and what use is that? Fire can't stop a fire.*

Or can it?

Her eyes widened. *Of course!* On the *Newsround* programme she'd seen about summer fires, the firefighters had stopped the fires by lighting smaller ones just ahead of the main blaze. The small fires had burnt away the vegetation so that when the main fire had reached the burnt areas there was nothing to fuel it and the fire had died down.

Lucy scanned the woods. The flames were approaching an open area of bracken. Beyond the bracken was a grove of old oak and horse chestnut trees, their massive trunks twisted into different shapes. *Maybe I could stop the fire before it reaches the trees*, Lucy thought, flying towards the bracken, her heart pounding. *If I start four or five small fires then make them die down when they've burnt the bracken away then the fire won't have anything left to burn . . .*

She hesitated. What if she couldn't control them? What if they just joined with the main fire and made things worse?

A young silver birch tree creaked and crashed to the forest floor, sending a shower of sparks spraying in every direction. Swerving to avoid them, Lucy pushed the worries out of her mind.

It wasn't a question of *could* she do it, she *had* to!

Lucy glanced up at the stars. *Help me,*

please, she thought. The sparkling light shone down and Lucy felt her panic slowly ebb away. She could do this. She *could* control her magic. Looking down at the bracken she decided she would light four fires across the path of the main fire.

She raised her arms. As she did so, Xanthe's words came back to her. *Just believe you can do it.*

'Fire,' she whispered, as her fingers started to tingle. 'Fire be with me.'

She pointed at the bracken. A ball of fire exploded from her fingers and the dry bracken blazed. As the flames shot upwards Lucy felt a flicker of panic but she forced it down. She waited until it had burnt an area of the clearing away and then, reaching out her hands again, focused with all her might on the fire. 'Fire be gone!' she cried.

She gasped. Her breath felt as if it were being sucked out of her. Fighting against the urge to panic, she forced herself to keep looking at the fire. 'Be gone!' she shouted.

The fire began to fade and as it did Lucy felt power flowing through her. Staring at the flames she imagined them getting smaller and smaller and gradually they died down until they were barely flickering. 'Be gone!' she whispered and they vanished. She'd done it! She'd controlled the fire with her mind! Excitement raced through her, but she didn't have time to waste. She swung round to another area of bracken and raised her arms again. 'Fire be with me!'

Four times she started a fire and then made it fade away. As she faded the fourth fire to nothing, she looked around. The clearing where the bracken had been was now bare and charred, covered by a layer of smoke. Not an inch of dry vegetation remained. Lucy's gaze flew to the main fire. It was almost at the edge of the blackened clearing. Had she burnt enough of the vegetation away to stop it?

Her heart beat anxiously as she watched the sparks falling on the burnt ground. They flickered and went out! The flames of the fire licked at the edges of the clearing but, finding nothing to burn and feed on, they simply got smaller and smaller and faded away.

I've done it! Lucy thought in delight as she watched the fire getting smaller and smaller. I've stopped it!

The area of wood burnt by the fire was blackened and mostly destroyed, with only a few of the taller trees left standing.

Lucy swooped closer to investigate the damage but as she reached the edges of the fire, there was a creaking noise. Lucy looked up in alarm. A nearby silver birch tree, its trunk burnt through, was falling into the clearing – and it was coming straight towards her!

Lucy shot up into the sky but she was just too late. Although the trunk of the tree missed her, one of its burning branches struck her shoulder as it fell. Crying out in pain, she crashed to the ground, landing with a thud among the leaves and branches of the fallen tree.

For a moment she lay there, feeling

dazed and breathless. Gradually the world stopped spinning and, pushing the leaves off her face, she tried to sit up. Pain shot across her shoulder and through her left ankle. She gasped and sank back down. She'd really hurt herself. She lay there for a moment. What was she going to do now?

Suddenly she heard a faint crackle behind her. Ignoring the pain that stabbed through her, she forced herself up on her elbows and looked around. The topmost branches of the fallen tree had fallen right on the spot where her last fire had been and flames were flickering through them. Lucy stared in horror. She couldn't have put the fire out completely and the flames were heading straight towards her!

CHAPTER

Ten

Lucy tried to stand but her ankle was too
painful. She cried out and collapsed back
into the leaves. She was too badly injured
to fly. Behind her the crackling grew
louder.

Her heart raced. What was she going to
do? Using every bit of strength in her
body, she fought against the pain that was
rising inside her. She had to concentrate.

It was *her* fire. She *could* control it.

Pain washed over her but Lucy forced herself to ignore it. 'Fire,' she gasped, making herself stare into the flames, 'be gone!'

The air seemed to rush out of her lungs. She felt weak. She wanted to give up, to cry out, but she gritted her teeth and forced herself to concentrate harder and harder. *I can do this*, she thought. *I can!*

'Lucy!' She heard a shout overhead but she ignored it.

Drawing on every ounce of willpower she possessed, she opened her mouth. 'Be gone!' she shouted.

The flames flared up a few centimetres away from Lucy's dress and then rapidly they faded and died.

Overcome with relief, Lucy collapsed

back, crying out as her shoulder hit the ground. Her head swam and for a moment the world seemed to fade away.

'Lucy! Lucy!' She heard a frantic voice shouting her name.

She blinked her eyes open and saw Allegra flying down towards her. 'Faye! Ella!' Allegra yelled. 'Over here!' She landed beside Lucy on the blackened earth. 'What's happened? Are you all right?' The words tumbled out of her.

'I–I'm OK.' Lucy managed to say. 'The fire. Has it all gone?'

Allegra looked around. 'Yes. What's been going on?'

Before Lucy could reply, Ella and Faye landed next to her.

'Lucy, you're hurt!' Faye said in alarm.

'It's my ankle and my shoulder,' Lucy

replied. Feeling sick, she shut her eyes.

'One of us should get help,' Ella said quickly.

'I'll go,' Allegra offered and a second later she was gone.

Lucy nodded and then groaned as her shoulder jarred against the hard ground.

'Don't talk for the moment,' Faye told her. She looked at Ella. 'I wish there was something we could do.'

'I could make the ground softer,' Ella suggested. She pointed to the ground around Lucy. 'Earth be with me, grass grow!'

Within seconds, soft thick grass was shooting up under and around Lucy, cushioning her against the hard ground. Its cool strands soothed her burnt skin. Immediately she felt more comfortable.

'Would you like some water?' Faye asked.

Lucy nodded and Faye quickly conjured a small raincloud nearby. She caught some of the rain in her cupped hands and carried it over to Lucy to sip.

As the cold clear water slipped down Lucy's throat she began to feel better. She smiled gratefully at Ella and Faye. 'Thanks.'

'So what happened?' Ella asked.

Lucy told them. 'I thought the fire was going to get me,' she finished. 'It was so close and I couldn't get away.'

'Oh, Lucy,' Faye said with a shiver.

'You did brilliantly to put it out,' Ella said admiringly.

'I'm glad you came along,' Lucy said. 'What were you doing in this bit of the woods anyway? Why weren't you in the clearing?'

'We were coming to see where you were,' Faye told her. She exchanged looks with Ella. 'Allegra told us about today – the ear-piercing and the stuff about you thinking we were going off together – so when it got late and there was no sign of you we thought maybe you'd decided not to come out tonight after all.'

'We were coming to try and persuade you,' Ella said.

'I was late because my dad watched a film, that's all,' Lucy told them.

Just then, Allegra swooped down from the sky.

'We're back!' Allegra cried. She was closely followed by Xanthe, Adam and Laura, an adult spring spirit who was wearing a green dress.

'Oh, Lucy,' said Xanthe, kneeling beside her. 'What has been going on?'

Lucy took a deep breath and told her story all over again.

'So you stopped the forest fire?' Xanthe said, as she finished. 'With your own fires?'

Lucy nodded. 'I lit four of them and managed to burn enough of the bracken away. Then I was knocked down and one caught light again.'

'And you still managed to put it out even though you were injured?' Adam said.

'Yes.' Lucy replied wearily. She was feeling very tired, her ankle was aching and her shoulder was burning.

'That's amazing!' Laura said. 'You were very brave, Lucy.'

'If it hadn't been for you the damage could have been so much worse,' Adam said. 'Well done.'

Lucy tried to smile at the praise but it was hard. She was so tired and so sore. Every bone in her body felt as if it was aching and her shoulder was throbbing. A lump of tears swelled painfully in her throat. She swallowed hard.

Xanthe put a hand on her arm. 'Come on,' she said gently. 'Let's get you sorted out.'

Adam crouched beside her foot. He took her ankle in his hand. As his fingers closed around it, Lucy gasped in pain. 'It's broken,' Adam said.

Lucy gulped. She wasn't sure how she was going to explain a broken ankle to her mum and dad.

'It's all right,' Xanthe said, seeming to

read her thoughts. 'Adam can fix it. He's a winter spirit, which means that as well as having the power to purify, he can heal wounds.'

Adam nodded and, closing his eyes, he held Lucy's ankle very still. A warm tingling sensation began to spread through Lucy's foot. It felt almost like pins and needles. Very slowly the tingling feeling faded until there was just a pleasant soothing warmth and then Adam took his hands away. 'It's mended,' he said. 'Try moving it a bit.'

Lucy gingerly wiggled her foot. To her surprise it didn't hurt at all! 'It's OK!' she gasped.

Adam moved to Lucy's side and, propping her up, laid his hand on her shoulder. Once again she felt pins and

needles and then the heat faded away.

'All better,' he said, letting go of her. 'There's just a faint scar there now but that should fade in time.'

Lucy could hardly believe it. She got slowly to her feet. Nothing ached. In fact, as she stretched her arms she realized that even her tiredness had left her. She felt light and full of energy. 'Wow!' she exclaimed, spinning round. 'I feel great.'

'That's cool!' Allegra said. 'I wish I was a winter spirit.'

'Will I be able to do that?' Faye asked Xanthe eagerly.

'Maybe one day,' Xanthe smiled. 'If you work hard at practising your magic.'

'Speaking of which,' Laura said, 'we should clear up here and get back to the feast.' She looked at Allegra, Faye and Ella. 'I thought Xanthe said that the three of you were supposed to be showing off your magic skills.'

'Can Lucy show hers off too?' Allegra asked Xanthe. 'She can control her magic really well.'

Lucy looked hopefully at Xanthe.

Her heart sank as Xanthe shook her head. 'I think Lucy's done enough for tonight. Besides,' Xanthe smiled, 'there's no need.'

Lucy looked at her in confusion. 'What – what do you mean?'

Xanthe looked at her. 'Lucy, you conjured four fires and put them out, stopping a serious forest fire. I think you've shown yourself more than ready to learn more about your magic.'

Adam and Laura nodded.

Lucy stared. 'So I can learn how to use my higher powers?' she asked, unable to quite believe it.

'You can,' Xanthe said.

'Oh, Lucy, that's brilliant!' Allegra squealed, hugging her.

Lucy hugged her back in delight.

★

It didn't take them long to sort out the
clearing. Ella helped Laura regrow the
bracken, brambles and trees. Faye and
Adam conjured rainclouds to water the
new plants and Allegra and Xanthe
conjured a breeze to blow away the
remains of the smoke. Soon the wood was
peaceful once again and, as the animals
and birds started to return, they all headed
back to the secret glade.

The clearing was full of stardust spirits.
Lucy had never seen so many in one place
before. They thronged across the grass or
perched in the branches of the trees
chattering and laughing, glowing fireflies
flickering around their heads. Near the edge
of the clearing four adult stardust spirits
were playing some very bouncy music that
seemed to call people to come and dance.

Around the base of the ancient oak tree a wooden table had been set up, piled high with food – bowls of strawberries, cherries and raspberries, plates of cakes, iced biscuits in the shapes of squirrels, mice and birds and huge jugs of pink lemonade.

'That's where we've got to show our magic off,' Allegra said, pointing to a space in front of the table.

Lucy saw Faye nervously touch her purple earrings. 'What if it all goes horribly wrong?' she said.

'It won't,' Lucy reassured her. 'You'll be great.'

Faye smiled. 'I'm glad you're here. It was horrid when we thought you might not be coming.'

Allegra and Ella nodded.

Lucy felt a rush of happiness. 'Thanks

for coming to find me,' she told them. 'If you hadn't come along when you did, I don't know what I'd have done.'

'Bet you'd have thought of something.' Allegra grinned. 'You're amazing, Luce. I can't believe you put out that fire — all on your own.'

'And you didn't even have your star stone,' Ella said.

'Just think what you could do if you had one,' Allegra said.

'I wish I could find out,' Lucy said with a sigh

Allegra, Ella and Faye exchanged looks. 'Well,' Allegra said, 'maybe you can.'

'Allegra! Faye! Ella!' Xanthe called from the oak tree. 'It's almost time.'

'Just a minute!' Allegra called. She looked at Lucy and from the pocket in her dress drew out a small package wrapped in gold tissue paper. 'This is your surprise, Luce. We were going to give it to you at the feast.'

Lucy took the present and pulled the tissue paper apart. Inside was a small chain of gold with two small pieces of onyx set on either side of it. They were earrings but they had been adapted to fit beautifully into the chain.

'It's an ankle chain,' Faye said. 'Xanthe asked Taryn to make it out of the earrings. It was Allegra's idea. You can wear it when you're flying.'

'Do you like it?' Allegra said anxiously.

Lucy held the two pieces of onyx. Warmth flooded through her fingers and up her arms. Her face broke into a huge grin. 'I love it!' she exclaimed.

They all grinned at her.

'Allegra!' Xanthe called again.

'Coming!' Allegra looked at Lucy. 'We'd better go!'

'Good luck!' Lucy cried.

As Allegra, Faye and Ella flew over to the oak tree, Lucy flew to a nearby horse chestnut and settled down amongst its leafy green branches. She put on her ankle chain. The two small black and white stones glinted in the starlight. Leaning her head against the tree's broad trunk, Lucy felt perfectly happy. She had the best three friends in the world.

Allegra, Ella and Faye came and stood in the middle of the clearing and, as the flutes played, they showed off their magic. Ella conjured a patch of willowherb, making the tall spikes of pink flowers

spring out of the soil in the shape of a star.
Faye called a raincloud, making it rain over
the flowers so their green leaves glistened
with drops of water and then Allegra
called a light breeze that delicately dried
the drops before fading away to nothing.

Coming to join them in the centre, an
adult stardust spirit announced that all
three of them were going to be allowed to
learn how to use their higher powers.

Utter delight rushed through Lucy.
Now they could all learn together!

As Lucy joined in the applause, she saw
Allegra, Faye and Ella touch their earrings.
She looked down at her own onyx ankle
chain. The stones glowed darkly.

She smiled. It was wonderful to have
her star stones and not to be the odd one
out any more, but deep down she knew

that, lovely as they were, she didn't really need them.

Fighting the fire that evening had shown her that Xanthe was right. Her ability to do magic didn't come from the stones. It came from inside her. She just had to believe in it.

I believe, she thought. *I really do.*

And with a smile she flew down to join the others.